OXFORD
UNIVERSITY PRESS

Great Clarendon Street, Oxford, OX2 6DP

Oxford University Press is a department of the University of Oxford.
It furthers the University's objective of excellence in research, scholarship,
and education by publishing worldwide in

Oxford New York

Auckland Bangkok Buenos Aires Cape Town Chennai
Dar es Salaam Delhi Hong Kong Istanbul Karachi Kolkata
Kuala Lumpur Madrid Melbourne Mexico City Mumbai Nairobi
São Paulo Shanghai Taipei Tokyo Toronto

Oxford is a registered trade mark of Oxford University Press
in the UK and in certain other countries

British Library Cataloguing in Publication Data available

ISBN 0-19-279091 9 (hardback)
ISBN 0-19-272543 2 (paperback)

3 5 7 9 10 8 6 4 2

Printed in Malaysia

N COJ

WITHDRAWN

Chicken
Licken

Ian Beck

OXFORD
UNIVERSITY PRESS

Once upon a time, when the world was young and the animals could speak, there was a tiny wee chick called Chicken Licken. Now it happened one day that fluffy, yellow Chicken Licken was grubbing about in her favourite patch, when an acorn fell, plomp, on her little tail.

'Oh no,' said Chicken Licken, 'the sky is falling down! Help, I must go and warn the king.'

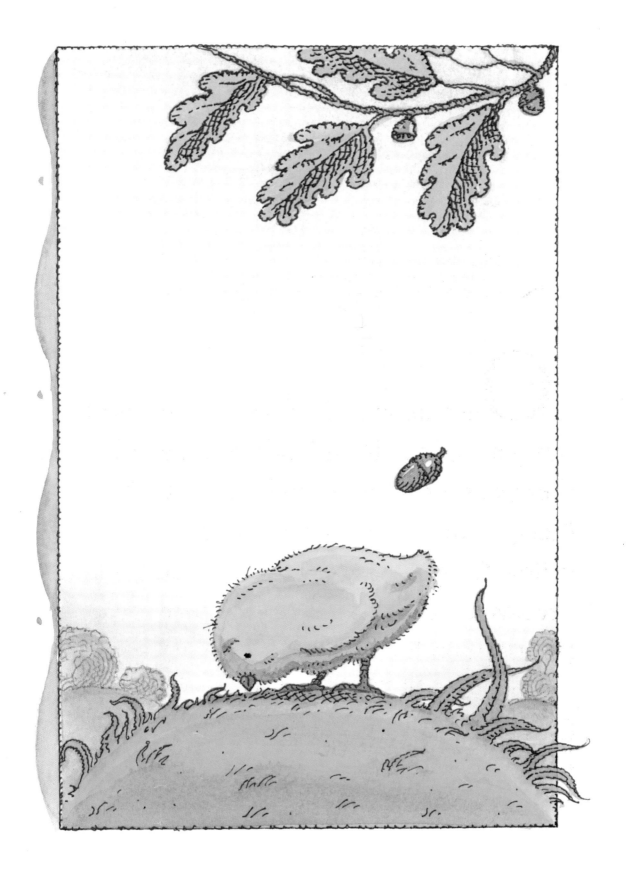

So she set off on her busy little feet, and after a while she met her great friend Henny Penny.

'Well, well, if it isn't Chicken Licken,' said Henny Penny. 'Where are you off to in such a hurry?'

'Quick, help, help, Henny Penny.

'The sky is falling down! I must go and warn the king.'

'I see,' said Henny Penny. 'And how can you be so sure that the sky is falling down?'

'Because,' said Chicken Licken, 'I saw it with my own two eyes, heard it with my own two ears, and a piece of the sky landed, plomp, on my own tail.'

'Then I'll come with you,' said Henny Penny. So they set off together, and tripped along through the grass until they met Cocky Locky.

'Well, a-doodle well,' said Cocky Locky to Henny Penny and Chicken Licken. 'Where are you two going, may I ask a-doodle do?'

'Oh, help, Cocky Locky,' said Henny Penny.

'The *sky* is falling down! We must go and warn the king.'

'I see,' said Cocky Locky. 'And how do you know the sky is falling a-doodle down?'

'Chicken Licken told me,' said Henny Penny.

'I saw it with my own two eyes, heard it with my own two ears, and a piece of the sky landed, plomp, on my tail,' Chicken Licken explained.

'Very well,' said Cocky Locky, 'I will travel with you, and we will warn the king.'

So all three set off skipping through the grass, until they met Ducky Daddles.

'Well, quack, well,' said Ducky Daddles.
'If it isn't Cocky Locky, Henny Penny, and
Chicken Licken. Where are you all off to?'

'Oh, help a-doodle do,' said Cocky Locky.

'The sky is falling down!

We must go and warn the king.'

'But how do you know the sky is falling
down?' asked Ducky Daddles.

'Henny Penny told me,' said Cocky Locky.

'Yes, and Chicken Licken told me,' said Henny Penny.

'I saw it with my own two eyes, heard it with my own two ears, and a piece of it landed, plomp, on my own tail,' said Chicken Licken once more.

'Then I had better, quack, come with you, and we can all warn the king,' said Ducky Daddles.

So they set off together, on their brisk little feet, until they met Goosey Loosey.

'Good morning to you, Ducky Daddles, Cocky Locky, Henny Penny, and Chicken Licken. Where are you going in such a rush?' asked Goosey Loosey.

'Oh help, Goosey Loosey,' said Ducky Daddles.

'The sky is falling down!

We must go and warn the king.'

'But how do you know that the sky is falling down?' asked Goosey Loosey.

'Cocky Locky told me,' said Ducky Daddles.
'Henny Penny told me,' said Cocky Locky.
'Chicken Licken told me,' said Henny Penny.

'And I saw it with my own two eyes, and heard it with my own two ears, and a piece of it landed, plomp, on my own tail,' said Chicken Licken.

'I'd better come with you, and together we can all warn the king,' said Goosey Loosey.

So they all set off in a busy little line, until they met Turkey Lurkey.

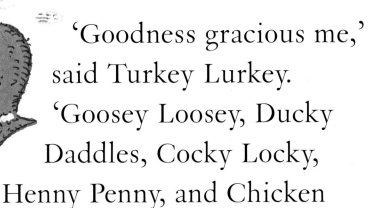

'Goodness gracious me,' said Turkey Lurkey. 'Goosey Loosey, Ducky Daddles, Cocky Locky, Henny Penny, and Chicken Licken! What a fine feathered sight on such a morning. Where are you all trotting off to?'

'Oh, you must help us, Turkey Lurkey,' said Goosey Loosey.

'The sky is falling down!

We must go and warn the king.'

'But how do you know the sky is falling down?' said Turkey Lurkey.

'Ducky Daddles told me,' said Goosey Loosey.

'Cocky Locky told me,' said Ducky Daddles.

'Henny Penny told me,' said
Cocky Locky.

'Chicken Licken told me,'
said Henny Penny.

'I saw it with my own two
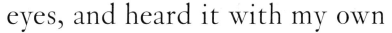
eyes, and heard it with my own
two ears, and a piece of it
landed, plomp, on my own
tail,' said Chicken Licken.

'I think I had better come
with you. Yes, that's the best
thing, then we can all warn
the king together,'
said Turkey Lurkey.

So off they all went,
smallest in front,
biggest at the back,
until they met
Mr Foxy Woxy.

'Mmmm, good morning,' said Mr Foxy Woxy. 'Well, well, well, if it isn't Turkey Lurkey, Goosey Loosey, Ducky Daddles, Cocky Locky, Henny Penny, and Chicken Licken. Where are you all going on such a fine morning?'

'Oh help, Mr Foxy Woxy,' they all said. **'The *sky* is falling down!**

We must go and warn the king.'

'But how do you know the sky is falling down?' asked Mr Foxy Woxy.

'Goosey Loosey told me,' said Turkey Lurkey.

'Ducky Daddles told me,' said Goosey Loosey.

'Cocky Locky told me,' said Ducky Daddles.

'Henny Penny told me,' said Cocky Locky.

'Chicken Licken told me,' said Henny Penny.

'I saw it with my own two eyes, and heard it with my own two ears, and a piece of it landed, plomp, on my own tail,' said Chicken Licken, nearly shouting by now.

'Then,' said cunning Mr Foxy Woxy, 'we shall all run together as fast as we can to my den, for safety, and then I will warn the king.'

So they all scurried on their busy little feet into the dark den of Mr Foxy Woxy.

And so it was that the king was never warned that the sky was falling down.

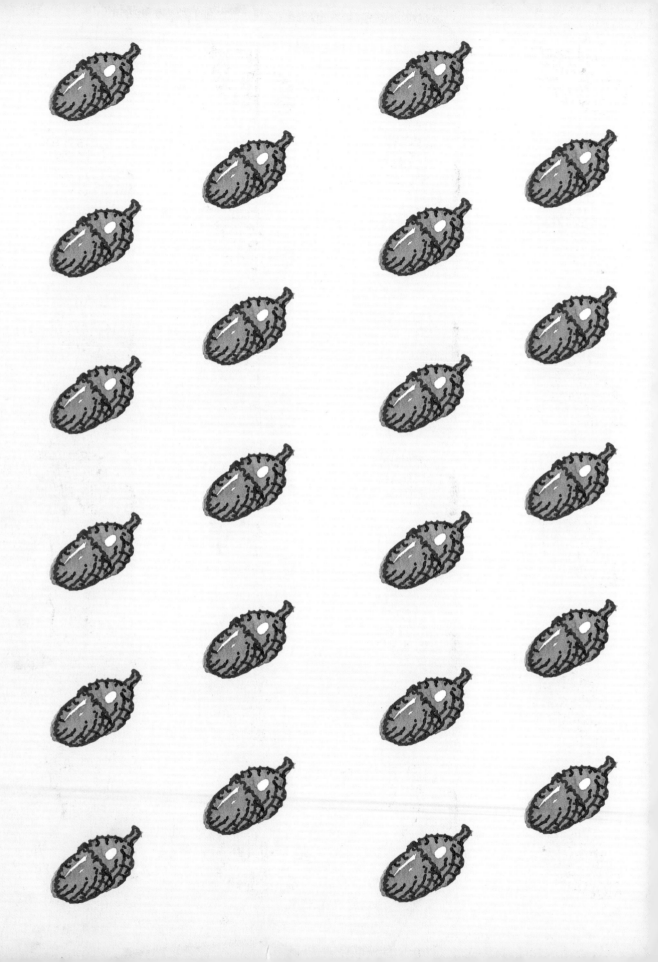